Dick Whittington
and his cat

©1985 Grandreams Limited.

First published 1985. This edition published 1990.

Written and illustrated by Anne & Ken McKie

Published by
GRANDREAMS LIMITED
Jadwin House, 205/211 Kentish Town Road, London, NW5 2JU.

Printed in Belgium.

ISBN 0 86227 813 9

KM1-4

Long, long ago in a little English village, lived a poor boy called Dick Whittington. He was all alone since his mother and father died. Dick had little money and often went hungry.

Now the boy often heard (from strangers passing through the village) that the streets of London were paved with gold. So, one day, Dick made up his mind to go and see for himself.

Early one morning, before the sun was up, Dick set off for London to seek his fortune.

He walked all morning until he came to the wide road that led to the city. A jolly man with a horse and cart offered him a ride.

"It's a long walk to London town, lad! Over a hundred miles!" shouted the man. Poor Dick's face fell, he had no idea it was so far.

The journey to London took many days and Dick was grateful for the ride. At last, one evening, as Dick drove the cart to the top of a hill, he spied the city of London far in the distance.

So many houses, so many streets and so many church towers. Soon they crossed London Bridge and the jolly man with the cart went his own way. As for Dick, he rushed off to find if the streets really were paved with gold!

He searched and searched until it was dark, but of course he found none. Then, very tired and very hungry, he fell asleep in someone's doorway.

What a shock Dick had the following morning! Instead of waking up to the birds singing, he woke up to the noise of the city. People scurrying about arguing and yelling. Some carrying all manner of goods and shouting their wares in the street. Wagons rattling by - horses - dogs - even sheep - but most of all, lots of people!

Dick just sat and stared. All at once, a door opened behind him. A great big hand reached out and grabbed him by the ear. "Get out of this doorway, you good-for-nothing boy," yelled the angriest woman Dick had ever seen. "This is the house of Mr. Fitzwarren," she screamed at Dick, and promptly threw him into the muddy street. "He's due back any minute. And I don't want him to find you lying on his doorstep."

Luckily for Dick, Mr. Fitzwarren was just crossing the street. He was a kind man and felt sorry for the poor boy. "Come, come, Cook," he said to the angry looking woman. "I'm sure you can find work for this lad in your kitchen. But first get him some food and fresh clothes."

    So that is how Dick Whittington came to be kitchen boy in the house of a wealthy merchant named Mr. Fitzwarren.

    How hard the bad-tempered cook made Dick work. All the day long he scoured the pots and scrubbed the black sooty pans. At night the cook made him sleep in an attic full of rats and mice. All night long they scampered around in the straw of Dick's bed. Some nights he got no sleep at all.

Every morning Dick went to the market to buy food for the cook to prepare. One day Dick found a stall that sold animals and birds.

"Will you sell me that cat for a penny?" the boy asked the stallholder, as he pointed to a box containing a beautiful cat. The woman took the penny and handed Dick his cat. "I shall call you Tibs!" the boy decided happily.

Soon, Tibs had got rid of every rat and mouse in the Fitzwarren house.

Alice, Mr. Fitzwarren's daughter, came down to the kitchen to thank Dick and his cat. She was delighted, for she hated rats!

Now, Mr Fitzwarren owned several ships that sailed from London, carrying goods to faraway lands.

Each time they sailed, the merchant asked his servants if they had any goods to sell in a distant land, and he would bring them back lots of money. Alas, Dick had nothing to send! "Send your cat," suggested Alice. "I am sailing with my father and I will look after her." Poor Dick felt he had to say "yes" to please Alice.

Dick stood waving on the quayside until the ship was out of sight. During the weeks that followed he was really lonely without Alice and Tibs the cat. All too soon the house was full of mice and rats again!

One night Dick decided to run away. Quietly, he slipped out of the house, and as he passed Bow Church - the bells began to ring, they seemed to say:

"Turn again, Whittington, Lord Mayor of London."

"I will turn again and I will become Lord Mayor of London!" And with that, Dick ran back to the Fitzwarren's house.

Faraway, over the sea, Mr. Fitzwarren's ship was in great trouble. The voyage had lasted weeks and weeks with no sight of land. Tibs the cat had made herself very useful and killed hundreds of rats and mice that swarmed all over the ship. Sad to say, the weather was getting much worse every day. The ship was pitching and rolling and enormous waves washed the deck. Not one of the crew was brave enough to climb the rigging to look for land. "This is the worst storm I have ever known," said Mr. Fitzwarren in despair. Alice began to cry. "If we don't reach land soon, we shall be drowned!"

Before anyone could stop Tibs, she climbed up to the top of the mast to look around. The ship was rolling in the gale, but Tibs hung on tight with her claws. By some miracle she managed to get safely back on deck. "Did you see land, Tibs?" demanded Mr. Fitzwarren. The cat nodded. "Was it far away?" cried Alice, and Tibs shook her head.

Knowing that land was ahead gave the sailors new hope. They all worked hard with the sails and the steering and gradually made it to the shore.

The people there had never seen a great sailing ship before. They made the Fitzwarrens and all the ship's crew very welcome, and took everyone straight to the Sultan's palace. The Sultan who ruled this land was very rich. His palace walls were studded with precious gems, and his tables and chairs were made of gold. He ordered a great feast to be prepared, and everyone from the ship was made welcome.

When all were seated around the golden table, the sultan clapped his hands for the servants to carry in the food. Row upon row of them came forward with heavy covered dishes made of gold. At a signal from the Sultan, the servants leaned forward and removed the covers. What a wonderful sight! Mouth watering meats and luscious fruits, they could hardly wait to begin.

Then it happened! Rats! Huge, fat, black rats! Shrieking and squealing, they swarmed all over the table. Soon, every scrap of food had vanished.

The Sultan wrung his hands in despair. "This happens at every meal. My kingdom is full of rats. My poor people have nothing left to eat!" He leaned across the golden table to Mr. Fitzwarren and Alice. "Look," he cried angrily, as he lifted up his foot. "They even chew our leather slippers." And he wriggled his toe through a big hole. "I would give half the treasure I own, to rid this land of rats!"

    Alice smiled at her father, for out of sight, under the table,
was Tibs the cat!

    "Let go of the cat!" said Alice's father. Quick as lightning,
Tibs shot from beneath the table and pounced on the nearest rat.
She moved so fast she soon killed all the rats that swarmed across
the floor - in no time, every rat in the palace was dead.

    After a few days not one single rat was left in the whole of
the Sultan's kingdom. Tibs had killed them all!

In a little while, Mr. Fitzwarren told the Sultan that they must set sail for home. "We will return with lots of cats on our next voyage. So never again will you be plagued by rats!"

The Sultan was so grateful he filled the ship with as much treasure as it could carry.

What rejoicing there was when, at last, the ship sailed up the Thames. What tales Alice and her father had to tell!

"Come forward, Dick Whittington!" ordered the merchant. "It is because of your wonderful cat that we have brought back all this treasure. By rights, Dick, it all belongs to you!"

So Dick became a rich man and married Alice and lived happily ever after.

Just as the bells foretold, he became Lord Mayor of London and is remembered to this day